WIN ONE
FOR THE GEEZER

WIN ONE

With an Introduction by Garry Trudeau

A Note from Mike's Mom
A Statement by Mike's Wife
and a letter from Art Buchwald

BANTAM BOOKS
Toronto   New York   London   Sydney

FOR THE GEEZER

The Cartoons
of MIKE PETERS

WIN ONE FOR THE GEEZER

A Bantam Book / November 1982

Excerpts from "Mike Peters, Dayton's Boy Wonder" by Dan Geringer, which originally appeared in OHIO Magazine, copyright © 1981 by *Ohio Magazine*. Used by permission. All rights reserved.

Piece by Charlotte Peters, previously published in CLONES, YOU IDIOT, I SAID CLONES, copyright © 1978 by Mike Peters. Used by permission of the *Dayton (Ohio) Daily News*.

Letter by Art Buchwald, copyright © 1982 by Art Buchwald. All rights reserved.

Designed by Lurelle Cheverie

Library of Congress Catalog Card No.: 82-90325

ISBN 0-553- 01429-3

Published simultaneously in the United States and Canada

Bantam Books are published by Bantam Books, Inc. Its trademark, consisting of the words "Bantam Books" and the portrayal of a rooster, is Registered in U.S. Patent and Trademark Office and in other countries, Marca Registrada. Bantam Books, Inc., 666 Fifth Avenue, New York, New York 10103

PRINTED IN THE UNITED STATES OF AMERICA

0 9 8 7 6 5 4 3 2 1

To my mom,
Charlotte Peters—
the First Lady
of St. Louis television

Introduction by Garry Trudeau

One of those things being remarked upon in professional circles these days is how many young editorial cartoonists are trying to draw like Mike Peters. No one is more amazed by this than Peters himself, who grew up wanting to draw like Bill Mauldin. Fortunately, he failed, spectacularly, and was forced by circumstance to develop an inimitable style of his own. All of us are the richer for it, especially Mike.

Fame and fortune hit Mike Peters like a freight train; one day he was just a struggling Dayton, Ohio, cartoonist living in a modest suburban ranch home, the next day he was a struggling Dayton, Ohio, cartoonist living in a modest sub- urban ranch home with a brand-new electric lawnmower parked outside. There was a period after he won the Pulitzer when Peters put on airs, when he dropped out of the car pool and began missing practice down at the Beaver-Vue Bowling Lanes, but his friends and neighbors now generally refer to it as "Mike's Hollywood period," a few dark weeks in the spring of 1981 when he temporarily forgot where he'd come from. According to his wife, who was in the room at the time, fame had caused Peters to peer into the unlit crevasses of his soul, and what he had seen there had not been very pretty. He described it to me once, and even I, a good friend, had to turn away in embarrassment. Later I called the police.

Actually, Mike wasn't really cut out for the fast lane anyway, especially since he never uses his blinkers. Mike is the Peter Pan of the cartooning world; he's boyishly charming, he's good with a rapier, and he doesn't spend a lot of time on the ground. Also, he doesn't seem to want to grow up, which is fine with those of us who love his work just the way it is. Mike Peters's cartoons are intelligent, funny and caring. How he gets them that way is his own business.

Garry Trudeau

A note from his mother

Mike was always a strange little boy. He was interested in everything, like dynamite caps, which he brought home after he took them off the railroad tracks to save the train from being derailed; at least that's what he told the police.

When he asked for a Superman outfit I made it for him. Do you think he played in it with other kids? Forget it! He wore it to school under his clothes, until the nuns chased him off the playground for stripping and running around in blue long johns. Superman was finally sent home by the principal for getting caught in the boys' room, leaping off a urinal at an unsuspecting janitor.

In high school, one of the Christian brothers took me aside and suggested that I send Mike to a vocational school since it was obvious that he was retarded. All he did was draw funny pictures! He never participated in any sports so we were thrilled when he went out for cheerleading. This would have been great except that Mike stuttered when he was in high school. And when he asked the cheering section to "G-g-g-give m-m-m-me a-a-a *C-C-C-C*," the whole section answered with a *"C-C-C-C."* They kicked him off the squad.

Mike and I have never seen eye to eye on certain things, like politics. I think it's terrible how Mike hounded Mr. Nixon out of office. And phone calls—he never calls me. I sit by the phone for days without eating so my mouth will not be full of food if the phone rings. But what do I treasure

most of all I possess? It's my boy! And this world
is a far, far better place than if he had entered
politics.

Charlotte Peters

A statement by his wife

Most cartoonists retain that childlike quality of seeing life all in black and white, without any gray areas. This provides a simple view of life which makes it easy to maintain ideals and retain the vigor of youth. Mike is all of these things and more.

There is also a side to Mike usually seen in maturity ages old. According to Eastern philosophy he is a very old soul. As a child his favorite toy was a broken hammerhead—solid and unbreakable—which imagination could transform into anything. He doesn't like cut flowers because they are already dead. He doesn't like birthdays or Father's Day because he thinks every day should be special. This lack of materialism makes his clothes situation a disaster. Recently, Mike announced that he needed a new wardrobe and promptly bought six new pair of jeans to replace the six old pair in his closet.

The most frequently asked question is, "How has the Pulitzer Prize changed our lives?" Mike is very fatalistic about success. He takes all the accolades in stride with the typical journalistic attitude that today's newspaper wraps tomorrow's fish. He concentrates on today's job, neither regretting yesterday, nor contemplating tomorrow. He is extremely conscientious about his work but everything else—checking accounts, electric bills, car oil—is extraneous.

Mike loves people. He sits down on a bus and tells the person next to him his life story and extracts secrets from total strangers. He has the ability to make people feel they have known him forever but, in fact, holds back a private part that no one knows. In that way, his private life is never in jeopardy no matter how much exposure he gets.

Marian Peters

WIN ONE
FOR THE GEEZER

How it all began...

When he returned from Vietnam, Mike Peters got a job on the art staff of the *Chicago Daily News,* where he struggled along anonymously until . . . one fine June day in 1968, Bill Mauldin, the *News*'s legendary editorial cartoonist, a two-time Pulitzer Prize winner who had befriended the young Peters in St. Louis and allowed the kid to sit around the *St. Louis Dispatch* office and watch him draw, walked into Peters's cubicle and said, "I just talked to an editor named Jim Fain in Dayton, Ohio, and I told him to hire you and he said he would."

"I finally met Fain in August," Peters says, "when he came to Chicago to cover the Democratic Convention. We're sitting in some hotel room, right off Lincoln Park, and the air-conditioning system is broken-down and all the windows and doors are open and the tear gas is coming in from everywhere. We're sitting there trying to conduct this interview with tears in our eyes. He never did see any of my cartoons. He could hardly see *me.* I said, 'I'd like to send you some of my work.' He said, 'It doesn't matter. If Bill says you're okay, you're okay.' That was my job interview.

"The last day before I left Chicago to come to Dayton, Bill Mauldin and John Fischetti came into my cubicle and said, 'Mike, now that you're one of us, we'd like to take you out to lunch.' And, of course, it was the proudest day in my life because there are only one hundred twenty editorial cartoonists in the *country,* and suddenly

I was one of them. And, y'know, editorial cartoonists don't grow up to be editors. I mean, no matter how good you get, you're not gonna be an editor. You don't *want* to be an editor. You just want to become an old editorial cartoonist. So they were like *initiating* me, and this was the only promotion I was ever gonna *get*.

"And, y'know, have you ever had one of those days where you're just totally *full* of yourself? This was my day. So we got on the elevator and the three of us *editorial cartoonists* went downstairs and we went over to Ricardo's and sat at the *editorial cartoonists'* table, y'know, and we had *editorial cartoonists'* drinks, and we sat around talking about *editorial cartoons.*

"And about halfway through lunch, it suddenly dawned on me that I was gonna be leaving my family behind until I was settled, getting on a bus, and going to Dayton to be an editorial cartoonist. And I said to Mauldin, 'What am I really supposed to *do* in Dayton as an editorial cartoonist? I don't really have any idea what my main function is. Am I supposed to make people laugh or cry or what?' And he said, 'There's only one thing an editorial cartoonist should be. He should be *mean.* He's supposed to *piss people off.*' And I said, 'Thanks. That's great. Piss people off. That's what I'm gonna do.'

"So I get on the bus the next day and it's a six-hour ride from Chicago to Dayton and I have all these editorials with me and I'm trying to rev myself up to get mean. I used to have a dog named Toni and Toni was very old. The only exercise she would get is when I would get her next to a door and say, 'Okay, Toni, why don't you go out there and *sic 'em*?' And Toni would start going, 'Aaaargh.' And I'd say, 'When you get outside there, Toni, I want you to *rip 'em apart.*' And Toni would go, 'Aaaargh. Aaaargh.' And when I really had her worked up, I'd throw open the door and scream, *'Kill 'em, Toni; kill 'em!'* And Toni would go *'Aaaargh!'* and run for about twenty feet and come back exhausted and very proud, and that would be her exercise for the day.

"So I was gonna work myself up the same way, and by the time I got to Dayton, after reading editorials for six hours and jotting down ideas that really ticked me off, I was *mad.* I got off that bus like the guy who gets off the stagecoach all dressed in black, wearing squeaky gloves, and he's kinda looking around, y'know? I felt like I had two pens strapped on either side of me and my spurs were kinda jinglin' in the dust.

"So I get off at this terrible bus depot they used to have in Dayton, and I look over and see all this graffiti on the walls. And I say, 'Boy, those cruddy *punks.* Somebody should *do* something about that.' And then I walk over to get my luggage and there's a bum asleep next to the luggage department and I say, 'Look at that *bum.* We shouldn't have *bums* here in Dayton, Ohio. I'm gonna *do* something about these bums.' And I get my luggage and leave the depot and cross Monument Avenue and I'm stepping up on the curb when I hear this voice say, 'Hold it there, buddy.'

"And I look around and there are two cops standing there. And one of 'em says, 'We got crosswalks here, y'know. You crossed in the middle of the street. I'm gonna have to write you up.' Now you gotta realize that, first of all, I was *mad.* I had worked myself up for six hours and I was *pissed off.* And second of all, I was now an *editorial cartoonist* and I knew they had run a story about me in the *Dayton Daily News* that day, y'know, 'MIKE PETERS COMES TO DAYTON,' and I thought I was *hot stuff.* I mean, I was gonna clean up this town and here were these two *cops* writing me up for *jaywalking.*

"So I put my luggage down and I say, 'Y'know, you boys are making a big mistake.' And they say, 'What?' And I say, 'I'm *Mike Peters.*' And the one cop says, 'Okay, Mike.' And he starts writing, 'M-i-k-e P-e-t-e-r-s.' And I say, 'I'm the new editorial cartoonist of the *Dayton Daily News.*' And he's writing, 'D-a-y-t-o-n . . .' I could see I was not exactly getting through. So I say, 'You guys have lots of *crime* here in Dayton, Ohio?' And they say, 'Yeah. Yeah, we do.' And I say, 'And I come in from Chicago, carrying my luggage, obviously new here, and you're giving me a ticket for *jaywalking*? In Chicago, you can sleep on the *street* and nobody cares.' And the one cop says, 'Sorry, buddy; you break the law, you gotta pay.'"

When Peters reported for work the next day, he was still furious. Editor Jim Fain welcomed him and showed him around. But Peters's mind was still reviewing the events of the previous evening, searching for a way to translate them into a devastating visual. The following day, drawing his first editorial cartoon for the *Daily News,* he found it. "I drew a bunch of delinquents, the black-jacket guys, stealing the wheels off a *bloodmobile,*" he says, grinning fiendishly. "They have the bloodmobile up on jacks and they're stealing the wheels and rolling them away. Then I drew two guys breaking into a bank, and a guy mugging some little old lady, and a big sign above all this reading, 'Dayton Street.' And then I had two big cops standing there watching a little kid with Mickey Mouse ears crossing the street and playing with his yo-yo, and the one cop is shouting to the other: *A jaywalker! Get him!*"

The next day, Peters watched the edition containing his cartoon roll off the presses. Then he sat smugly in his office, knowing he had just infuriated the entire Dayton police force, waiting for the phone to ring. *They will think twice,* he thought, *before they mess with* Mike Peters *again.*

At 4:00 P.M., the phone rang. He will never forget the conversation. "I say, 'Hello?' And a voice says, 'This is Chief Igleburger of the Dayton Police Department.' And I say, real sarcastic,

'Well, Chief Igleburger of the Dayton Police Department, I guess you guys are *pretty mad* about the cartoon today, huh?' And he says, 'Oh no, I really thought it was cute. It showed we were doing our job, arresting people, and I'd like to have the original for my wall.' I was dumbfounded. It had *completely* gone over his head. He thought it was *cute.* And that was my introduction to Dayton, Ohio."

Not quite. Peters went upstairs to the composing room to retrieve his cartoon. He had no intention of hanging it on Chief Igleburger's wall, of course, but he did want to keep it himself. It was his first real editorial cartoon and it meant something to him. He couldn't find it in the composing room, so he went to engraving. "I couldn't find it there, either," he recalls, "so I said, 'Does anybody know where my cartoon is?'

Somebody said, 'Oh yeah, so-and-so threw it away over there.' I looked in the trash can. Somebody had taken my original cartoon, crushed it, and thrown it away. I exploded.

"Now, to understand what happened next, you have to know two things. First, they were used to getting syndicated cartoons, not originals, and they always threw them away after running them. Second, when I got hired here, the first thing Fain said was, 'Hey, it's not Mr. Fain, you call me Jim. We're a *family* here. We on the editorial board are a *family*.' And what I thought he was telling me was that I was an *editor,* a *boss.* I mean, I thought I was *management.*" He laughs uncontrollably at the thought.

"So I'm in the engraving department, holding my crushed original cartoon, and I am furious. I point to Clint Plummer, the foreman, and I say, 'Clint, get everybody around here. I have something to say.' And Clint looks startled and he says, 'What?' I say, 'Get everybody around here. *Now.*' So Clint gets everybody around me and they're all kinda looking at each other and I say, 'If *any* of you *ever* does this to my cartoon again, your ass is *grass.* Do you understand? I am speaking for Jim Fain now. Your ass is *grass.*' And I stomped out.

"Well, I'm back in my office, putting my cartoon together again and rubber cementing it down on cardboard and feeling real proud of myself when the phone rings and it's Marilyn Moomaw, Jim Fain's secretary, and she says, 'Mike, uh, Mr. Fain would like to talk with you,' and I say, 'Great, I've got something to tell Jim.' And I take the cartoon to Fain's office to show him what happened.

"I walk in and standing there, behind the desk, are Fain and Clint Plummer and another guy from the engraving department. And I come in and say, 'Well, Jim, did Clint tell you what his guys did?' And Fain says, 'Shut the door, you stupid idiot, and get over here.' And then he just tore me apart for the next thirty minutes." Peters assumes the narrative tone most often heard at the conclusion of a *Waltons* episode. "I realized then," he says solemnly, "that we were not a family after all. And that I would never get to call Fain 'Dad.'"

Adapted from
"Mike Peters, Dayton's Boy Wonder"
by Dan Geringer (*Ohio Magazine,* June 1981)

HIS FANTASY, TATTOO?... HE WANTS TO CUT TAXES, INCREASE DEFENSES AND BALANCE THE BUDGET ALL AT THE SAME TIME...

12

13

@1981 DAYTON NEWS

IT'S BEEN LIKE THIS SINCE THE CUT BACKS TO THE PERFORMING ARTS...

HE SAID "ABSOLUTELY NO HANDOUTS"... BUT, HE'D HELP US APPLY FOR A SMALL BUSINESS LOAN...

15

WHEN YOU SAID YOU WERE PUTTING TWO THOUSAND DOLLARS INTO IRA, I THOUGHT YOU MEANT A RETIREMENT ACCOUNT...

TELL ME, CHARLES... EXACTLY WHAT DO YOU KNOW ABOUT THIS GIRL?   17

RELAX... IT'S GOOD ENOUGH FOR GOVERNMENT WORK.

RALPH, I DIDN'T KNOW YOU CARED... A BRAND NEW PINTO AND WITH FIRESTONE 500'S.. 19

SO WHAT'S WRONG WITH RELEASING HARMLESS AMOUNTS OF KRYPTON GAS INTO THE ATMOSPHERE?..

WE ASKED MR. AND MRS. RALPH HICKS TO TEST OUR NEW DIOXIN PESTICIDE...
AND AFTER ONE YEAR THEY'RE HAPPY TO REPORT, NO PHYSICAL SIDE EFFECTS.

21

LAB

REMEMBER THE GOOD OLD DAYS WHEN WE ONLY HAD TO SMOKE A FEW CIGARETTES AND EAT SACCHARIN?

I CAN'T TAKE IT ANYMORE... THE BURGLARIES.. THE BREAK-INS.. RUNNING FROM THE COPS... HIDING OUT IN FLEA-RIDDEN MOTELS... CHARLIE, YOU'VE GOT TO QUIT THE **FBI**.

OFFICIAL CIA ASSASSINATION KIT.

A POISONED RING THAT EXPLODES WHEN YOU LIGHT IT

AN ORDINARY LOOKING FOUNTAIN PEN THAT CAUSES DEATH WHEN EATEN BY AN UNSUSPECTING VICTIM

A TRAINED SCORPION THAT EXPLODES WHEN A VICTIM TURNS ON CAR IGNITION

DEADLY TIME BOMB THAT KILLS INSTANTLY WHEN INJECTED IN THE BLOOD STREAM

POISONED CIGAR THAT BRINGS IMMEDIATE DEATH WHEN SECRETLY DROPPED IN VICTIMS DRINK

© DAYTON DAILY NEWS

26

27

FUNNY...I DON'T REMEMBER YOU AT THE NASA TRAINING CENTER...

29

THANK YOU, REVEREND ... AND NOW, IN COMPLIANCE WITH **FCC** ELECTION YEAR RULES, HERE TO SPEAK FOR THE OPPOSING VIEW IS...

31

33

34 "THEN IT'S SETTLED — HE GETS EASTERN EUROPE AND WE GET DETENTE, PARK PLACE AND MARVIN GARDENS...."

THINK... WHERE DID YOU GET THOSE CELLS WE'VE BEEN WORKING WITH?...

37

THE WARREN COURT

THE BURGER COURT

39

YOU'VE BEEN FOUND GUILTY OF BEING POOR, FEMALE AND RAPED.
AND WE SENTENCE YOU TO NINE MONTHS HARD LABOR...

This is Mary . . . She's underpaid, sexually harassed, passed over for promotion and stuck in a stereotyped role . . .

She's also against the ERA . . . why?

She likes being treated special . . .

STOP ERA

©DAYTON NEWS 1980

42

The Phyllis Schlafly Dress for Success Tips...

1. Gray pin stripe suit ①
2. White monogramed shirt ②
3. Silk tie ③
4. Brief case ④
5. Black Oxfords ⑤

© 1981 DAYTON DAILY NEWS

MEN

WOMEN

43

45

CLONES, YOU IDIOT...I SAID CLONES.

47

LOOK, LADY— YOU'RE THE ONE WHO ASKED FOR A FAMOUS MOVIE STAR WITH DARK HAIR, STRONG NOSE AND DEEP SET EYES...

48

I FEEL RIDICULOUS TOO...BUT WE'VE TRIED EVERYTHING ELSE...

49

IN RESPONSE TO THIS STATION'S EDITORIAL AGAINST THE SEXUAL EXPLOITATION OF CHILDREN IN ADVERTISING... HERE TO REPRESENT THE OPPOSING VIEW...

WE KNOW HOW TO STOP IT... BUT IT'S HARD TO FIND A VIRGIN AT A SKI RESORT...

51

YOU HEARD ME, CHIEF...
I FOUND A PICTURE
OF A FORMER
PRESIDENT ON AN
ALL MALE CRUISE
WEARING SILK
STOCKINGS AND A
POWDERED WIG.

PHONE

NATIONAL
ENQUIRER

53

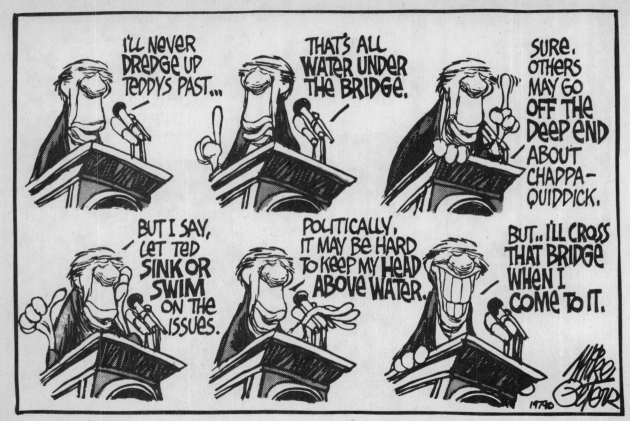

DAYTON DAILY NEWS 1976 ©

Mike Peters

55

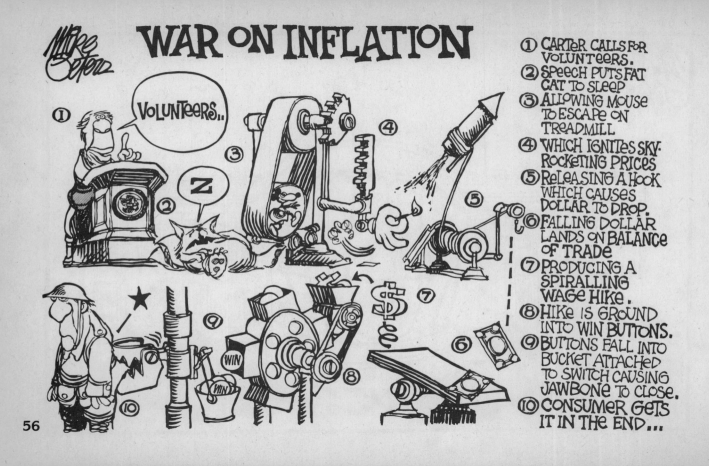

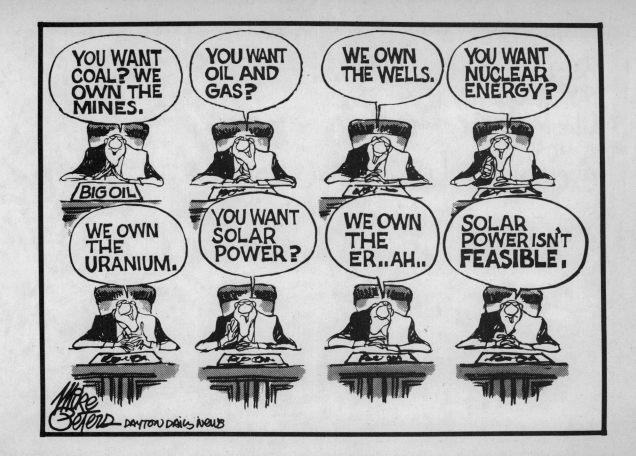

Carter Campaign Buttons..

© 1980 DAYTON DAILY NEWS

TIP-A-CANOE and mondale too ?

Two empty cars in every garage

THE BUCK DROPS HERE!

He kept US out of the Olympics

61

DAYTON DAILY NEWS 1790 *Mike Peters*

TOO OLD · Ronnie

TOO SLICK · BIG JOHN

TOO DULL · BUSH

TWO FACED · Brown

As a candidate ...this man would be against capital punishment, for social reforms, opposed to the arms race, in favor of the **ERA** and therefore unacceptable to the *Moral Majority* . . .

© 1980 DAYTON DAILY NEWS

ANOTHER hostage released...

©1981 DAYTON DAILY NEWS

64

We knew him as a glamorous movie star . . . but there was a side of him we never knew . . .

65

GIVE ME YOUR _TRULY_ TIRED, YOUR _TRULY_ POOR, YOUR _TRULY_ HUDDLED MASSES...

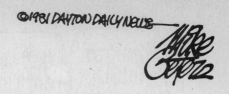

69

71

WATT

72

73

74

DON'T WORRY... I'M IN CHARGE HERE...

75

HE'S GROWN A FOOT SINCE I SAW HIM LAST....

THAT'S ODD...THEY'RE COOKED ALREADY...

THERE'S ANOTHER GROUP HERE COMPLAINING ABOUT OUR NEUTRON BOMB TESTING...

GOOD GOD..... IT'S GENE KELLY...

82

...THEN ONE DAY THE BRAVE AND HANDSOME HUNTER CAME UPON A CLEARING IN A WOODED GLADE...SUDDENLY HE RAISED HIS TRUSTY RIFLE AND TOOK CAREFUL AIM... BLAM, BLAM... HE DROPPED BAMBI AND BAMBI'S MOTHER... BLAM, BLAM... HE GOT THUMPER AND FLOWER... BLAM, BLAM, BLAM...

83

FOR GOD'S SAKE, PINOCCHIO... QUIT THAT JOB WITH THE NATIONAL ENQUIRER...

LOOK...I'M SORRY...I THOUGHT YOU GUYS SAID GOLD, FRANKINCENSE AND *MIRTH*...

OK, NOW TRY IT...

91

Here's the latest family killed by an IRA terrorist attack ...

Here's an IRA terrorist on a hunger strike ...

Guess which one will be called a martyr ...

HAVE YOU NOTICED THAT PICTURE HASN'T CHANGED IN TWO DAYS? 93

FRANKLIN SAID THIS IDEA WAS SENT TO HIM BY A YOUNG LAW
STUDENT FROM WHITTIER, CALIFORNIA...

95

THAT'S FUNNY...THE LOCK'S BEEN CHANGED...

It's a bird, It's a plane...

At 8:15 in the morning on November 7, 1979, Mike Peters, syndicated editorial cartoonist of the *Dayton Daily News*, dressed himself in a homemade Superman costume and perched on the third-floor ledge of the *Daily News* Building outside the window of former Governor Cox's library, fighting the cold and his fear of flying and the souvenirs of Dayton's exploding pigeon population scattered generously around his red-stockinged feet.

In forty-five minutes, he knew, the editorial board would solemnly convene in the governor's library to decide which stories to run in that afternoon's edition. The library, a throwback to the days when Governor Cox ran both the state and the newspaper, looked like a Victorian stage set—three walls lined with floor-to-ceiling walnut bookshelves stuffed with hundreds of worn volumes, wall-to-wall regal red floral-patterned carpet, a huge oak conference table surrounded by red plush armchairs, and two large windows facing east, covered by heavy, dark blue drapes. The window Peters stood behind was cracked open a few inches to allow him to hear the editors when they entered. The drapes hid him completely.

Peters's wife, Marian, had fashioned the Superman costume out of a blue ballet leotard, carefully sewing on the mandatory red shorts, the cape, the belt and the padded red *S* on a field of brilliant yellow. A pair of red stocking-slippers completed the ensemble. She had presented it to her thirty-six-year-old husband just prior to Halloween, and he had worn it proudly while trick-or-treating in his suburban Beavercreek neighborhood with his three children. A few days after Halloween, he had noticed it hanging forlornly in his closet, considered the amount of time that had gone into its creation, and pondered the metaphysical juxtaposition of illusion and reality. Slowly, a maniacal grin spread across his face.

Poised precariously on the ledge, Peters was securely hidden from the inside, but his presence outside had not gone undetected. Across the street, on the third floor of the Grant-Deneau office tower, a large flock of secretaries had gathered at the windows, waving to him and holding up handwritten messages. He could not read the messages, and he could not return the waves because he was clinging to the window for dear life.

Peters's life did not flash before his eyes, as is traditional in these situations. Instead, he remembered himself as a child, seemingly built out of pipe cleaners, stuttering uncontrollably, trying to survive the second grade at St. James, a parochial school in the rough Irish-German section of St. Louis known as Dog Town. Superman was both a comic book and a television star in those days, the idol of millions, including the fledgling Peters. So Charlotte Peters, star of her own television talk show in St. Louis and a perceptive mom to boot, bought a pair of button-up-the-back long johns, dyed them blue, and sewed her son a perfect replica of the Man of Steel's threads, featuring a huge *S* on the chest, padded like a pillow.

Little Peters immediately took the macho route, wearing the legendary ensemble underneath his school uniform, searching out the largest eighth-graders he could find, and urging them to smash him in his secretly padded chest.

After the schoolyard had resounded with their horrendous whomps for an appropriate period of time, Peters would tear open his shirt, simultaneously revealing the invincible *S* and his true identity while his would-be attackers stood around nursing their impotent fists.

After a while, Peters dispensed with the preliminaries entirely, took off all his school clothes, and swooped joyously around the schoolyard in his red stocking-slippers. This immediately caught the eye of an attendant nun, and she was not pleased. A cease-and-desist order was dispatched to Super Mom, but Peters was a sly little devil. Eschewing the schoolyard, he took to undressing in the boys' bathroom, perching in full regalia outside a window directly above the urinal, waiting until he heard the door open and close, then screaming *"Tant-ta-da!"* and landing smack in front of his startled prey.

Now, almost thirty years later, the moment was again at hand. Peters heard the editors enter the governor's library, seat themselves around the conference table, and start their meeting. He began opening the window. Suddenly, the meeting stopped, the library filled with silence, and the editors sat there listening to the window opening behind the drapes, wondering what the hell was going on.

Peters threw the drapes aside and leaped off the windowsill. "Sorry I'm late," he said, "but I had lousy weather over Cleveland." Then he walked quickly past the stunned editors, through the city room, and into his office.

"They still talk about that day," he says proudly.

(From "Mike Peters,
Dayton's Boy Wonder"
by Dan Geringer)

ART BUCHWALD

Dear Mike:

   Several people have sent me your cartoon about the dead robin.
In many places it appeared on the same day as my column. I would just
like to tell you that my lawyers are now working on the suit. I can prove
that I got the idea in January. I'd be willing to take it to arbitration in some
neutral town like Beirut or Jerusalem. Please check with me in the
future on all the cartoons you are doing and I will let you know if I have
already thought of the idea first. I talked to Jeff MacNelly about it the other
day, and he says you keep doing it to him all the time.

Cheers,

Art Buchwald

105

QUICK, READ ME THAT SUPREME COURT RULING ABOUT ALIENS ATTENDING PUBLIC SCHOOLS...

SORRY, HE CAN'T COME TO THE WATERGATE REUNION...
HE'S IN BED WITH A BUG...